Fireworks at the FBI

Capital Mysteries 6

by Ron Roy
illustrated by Timothy Bush

A STEPPING STONE BOOK™

Random House New York

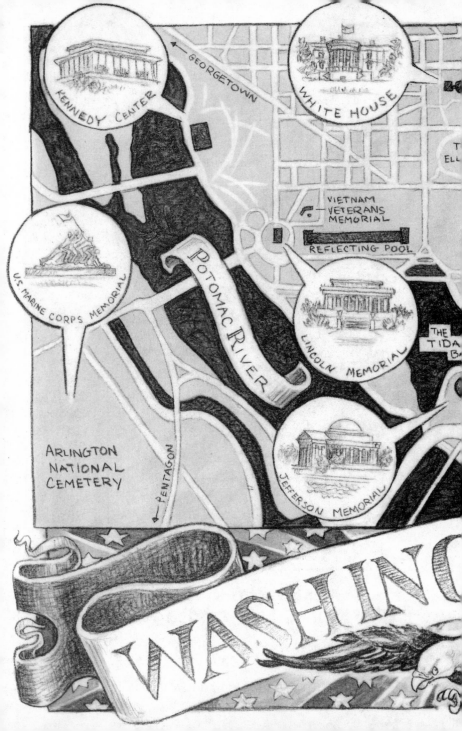

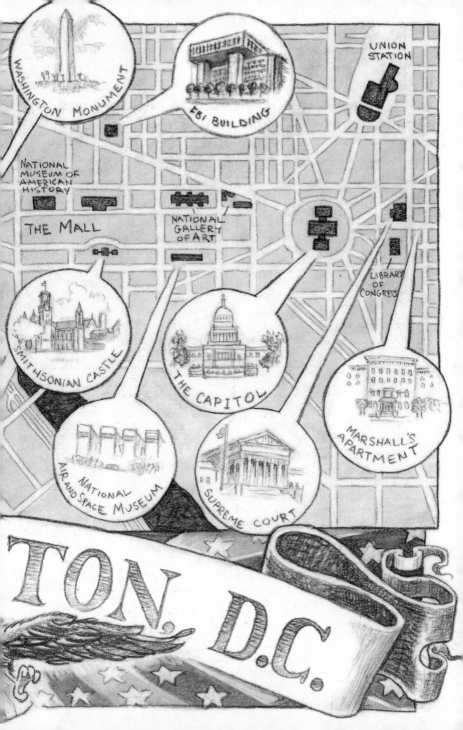

This book is dedicated to Lily, Ian, and Ryan—thanks for the chips.
—R.R.

Photo credits: pp. 88–89 courtesy of the Library of Congress.

www.randomhouse.com/kids
www.steppingstonesbooks.com

Educators and librarians, for a variety of teaching tools, visit us at
www.randomhouse.com/teachers

Library of Congress Cataloging-in-Publication Data
Roy, Ron.
Fireworks at the FBI / by Ron Roy ; illustrated by Timothy Bush. —
1st ed.
    p.   cm. — (Capital mysteries ; #6)
"A Stepping Stone Book."
SUMMARY: As they leave a Fourth of July celebration with the President of the United States, KC and Marshall see unauthorized fireworks at the FBI Building and decide to unmask the culprit and his plans for blackmail.
ISBN 0-375-87527-1 (pbk.) — ISBN 0-375-97527-6 (lib. bdg.)
[1. Extortion—Fiction. 2. United States. Federal Bureau of Investigation—Fiction. 3. Washington (D.C.)—Fiction. 4. Mystery and detective stories.] I. Bush, Timothy, ill. II. Title. III. Series: Roy, Ron, Capital mysteries ; #6.
PZ7.R8139Fir 2006 [E]—dc22 2005036068

Printed in the United States of America
10 9 8 7 6 5 4 3 2 1 First Edition

Contents

1
Runaway Rockets

A fiery ball exploded in the sky over the Washington Monument. Red, white, and blue sparks cascaded slowly down, high above the crowd.

The sparks twinkled, then winked out. "THAT'S ALL THERE IS, FOLKS," a man's voice boomed over a loudspeaker. "THANK YOU AND HAVE A HAPPY AND SAFE FOURTH OF JULY!"

Three thousand people clapped, whistled, and cheered.

"Those were the best fireworks I've ever seen!" the President of the United States said.

"And this is the best July Fourth!" said KC.

She and her best friend, Marshall Li, were watching the fireworks from the lawn in front of the Museum of Natural History. President Zachary Thornton and KC's mom, Lois, sat near them, holding hands. They had gotten married a few months ago.

"Shall we go home?" Lois suggested. "I think Yvonne made a cake for us."

"Awesome!" KC and Marshall said at the same time.

"Home" was the White House. KC, her mom, and KC's two cats had all moved in after the wedding. Marshall was staying at the White House for the holiday.

The president folded the blanket and

tucked it under his arm. Marshall carried the basket, and they walked toward a sleek black car parked nearby.

Six tall men in dark suits followed them. One of the men spoke quietly into a tiny microphone on his wristwatch. Wherever the president went, secret service men came with him. They protected him at all times.

"Can we walk back to the White House?" KC asked.

"Sure. I can use the exercise," the president said.

"But I like riding in the car," said Marshall. "When I learn to drive, I'll never walk anywhere!"

KC laughed. "Then your legs will shrivel up and you'll look like one of your spiders!"

Marshall was crazy about bugs and spiders. Sometimes he seemed to like them more than people.

The president handed the blanket to one of the six men, who put it in the car with the basket. Then they walked through the darkness toward the White House. The six men stayed close behind.

"It feels creepy having those guys following us," Marshall whispered to KC.

"That's what you get for hanging out with the president," KC joked.

They all said "Hi!" to a man walking a dog with long, skinny legs. The man's mouth fell open when he recognized the President of the United States.

"What kind of dog is this?" the president asked. He stroked the dog's ears.

"Manfred is a greyhound," the man

said. "I adopted him in Colorado before I moved out here. He used to race at a dog track."

"He seems very gentle," KC said.

The man smiled. "Greyhounds make great pets," he said.

After saying good night to the man and his dog, they started walking again.

"I should have a dog," the president said. "Then I'd get exercise when I walked him around the White House grounds."

"You could walk your cat," Marshall teased.

The president laughed. "I wonder if George would like that."

They passed several large buildings, all dark at nine-thirty on a holiday night.

Suddenly KC heard a whizzing sound

over their heads. She looked up just as a white flame shot out of one of the windows in a sprawling building. "Did you see that?" KC cried.

"It came out of the FBI building!" the president said.

"It looked like a rocket!" Marshall said.

As they stood there gaping, another rocket flew out through the window.

Right away the secret service men surrounded the president and his group. The president's car pulled up, and President Thornton, KC, her mom, and Marshall were shoved inside. Then the black car shot forward and streaked toward the White House.

KC pressed her nose against the window. All she saw was a blur.

In the backseat, the president yanked

out his cell phone and flipped it open. A moment later, he was talking to the director of the FBI, Desmond Smiley.

"We all saw it, Desmond!" the president said. "Lois and the kids were with me, and about half a dozen secret service agents. I'm telling you, fireworks shot out of one of the windows in the FBI building!"

The president listened. "Call me as soon as you know anything, no matter how late!"

He flipped his phone shut and slipped it back into his pocket.

"What happened?" KC asked. "Were they really rockets?"

"We don't know yet," the president said. "But Mr. Smiley will have the fire department check it out."

Within seconds, they heard sirens.

"Boy, that was fast!" Marshall said as the president's car zoomed inside the presidential garage.

The president, Lois, and the two kids slipped through a private entrance to the White House. The president greeted a few guards, then entered an elevator. KC's favorite marine guard, Arnold, saluted them as they stepped out.

"Were the fireworks exciting?" he asked.

"I'll say!" Marshall blurted, making KC laugh.

When they were inside the residence, KC dropped into a chair at the kitchen table. She realized she had hardly taken a full breath since they'd seen the rockets at the FBI building.

George, the president's cat, was lying in his bed near the stove. KC's cats, Lost and Found, were cuddled up with him.

Suddenly the phone rang. KC jumped. She felt like a coiled spring.

The president must have felt the same way. He answered on the second ring. "Yes?" he said.

The president listened, nodding his head.

"Pizza?" he asked. He sounded surprised. "Okay, good job getting there so fast, Chief."

"What about pizza?" Marshall asked after the president hung up.

"The fire department discovered which room those rockets were shot from," the president answered. "And they found a burning pizza box in a trash basket."

"Who shot off the rockets?" KC asked.

"The fire chief thinks it was an accident," the president said. "Apparently, someone left a package of rockets on the desk right above the trash basket. The chief thinks a spark from the fireworks celebration flew in through the open window and set the pizza box on fire, and the fire lit the rockets."

KC frowned. It seemed like an awfully big coincidence to her. But the president didn't seem bothered.

"My cousin had some rockets last year," Marshall said. "He told me they won't fly if they're lying flat when you light them. You have to set them in a special holder or stick them in the ground."

The president had been reaching for a glass of water. But he set it back down without taking a sip. He looked serious.

"Marshall, it sounds as if you're saying some person had to aim the rockets," the president said. "They wouldn't be able to launch themselves, even if a spark accidentally lit them. Right?"

Marshall nodded. "Right, sir."

"Why would anyone want to shoot rockets out the FBI window?" KC asked the president.

"I don't know," he answered. "I'm going to the FBI building in the morning. We may have some answers by then."

"Can Marshall and I go with you?" KC asked.

KC planned to become a Washington reporter after college. Deep down inside, KC felt this fireworks story was big, and she wanted to be in on it!

2

The Clue in the Trash Can

At ten the next morning, the president, KC, and Marshall left the White House for the FBI building. The black presidential car dropped them off in front of the broad marble steps.

A pair of marine guards came to attention outside the entrance. The two men reached for the doors and pulled them open.

"Thank you," President Thornton said as he and the kids entered.

The director of the FBI waited just inside, in the lobby.

He shook the president's hand. "The

fire chief is here already," Desmond Smiley said. He led the president and the kids through the lobby, past the guard's desk, to a small meeting room.

A large man in a blue suit stood up. "Good morning, Mr. President," he said.

"Good morning, Chief," the president said as everyone sat around a table. "What have you found out?"

"I believe someone deliberately shot those rockets but wanted to make it look like an accident," the fire chief said. He glanced at a small notebook. "They're called Zinger rockets, by the way."

"So this wasn't an accident?" the president asked.

"That's unlikely," the fire chief said. "A spark flying through that open window could have started the fire, but someone needed to hold the rockets in a position where they'd fly out that window."

KC felt Marshall kick her under the table. "I was right!" he hissed.

KC nodded but didn't answer. She wanted to hear what was being said.

"I think he used the metal trash basket as his launching pad," the fire chief was saying.

The president tapped a pen on the tabletop. He turned to the fire chief. "Was anyone in the building when your crew got there?" he asked.

"Yes, sir, a guard," the chief said. "Name of Joe Cellucci, worked in the building for sixteen years. He told us it was a normal Friday night, for a holiday, until the rockets started flying out the window."

"Who uses that office?" the president asked.

"Five secretaries," the director said.

"Did you question them?" the president asked.

"Yes," the director told him. "All long-time employees. When they left, the door was locked and the windows shut."

"And I'm guessing none of them admitted to bringing Zinger rockets into the office." President Thornton sighed.

"Right, sir," the director said. "If they are telling the truth, someone else came in after they left and fired the rockets. Why, I can't imagine, unless it was a Fourth of July prank."

The president stood up. "I would like to see the room where this all took place," he told the FBI director.

"Certainly," Desmond Smiley said. "Follow me, please."

The president and the kids followed the director to the lobby.

"Why doesn't Mr. Smiley ever smile?" Marshall whispered to KC.

KC shook her head. "Maybe he does when there's something to smile about!"

Mr. Smiley led them to a pair of elevators. They took one to the third floor. Mr. Smiley used a key to open an office several doors down the hall from the elevator. "This is where it happened," he said.

They all stepped into the room. KC saw five desks, five computers, and a wall of metal filing cabinets. Opposite the door were two windows. Under one sat a metal wastebasket with a red pizza box sticking out.

"EEEW! What's that smell?" KC asked. She wrinkled her nose.

"It's burned powder," the fire chief said. "From the rockets."

The president walked over and looked inside the trash can. He opened one of the windows, then picked up the can. He tipped it so the can's opening rested against the window ledge.

"Could someone have shot the rockets this way, Desmond?" the president asked.

"I think so, sir," the FBI director said. "The rockets would shoot straight out the window."

"Marsh, look at this!" KC cried excitedly. She pulled the red pizza box out of the can. One whole side was burned and blackened. Bits of the cardboard crumbled when she opened the lid.

"Empty." Marshall sighed. "Not even a piece of crust left."

"I suppose this will be one of those unsolved mysteries," the president said. "We'll never know for sure why someone fired rockets from this room."

KC shot Marshall a look. She was sure something weird was going on here. And there was something about that pizza box that bothered her. . . .

"Ready to go, kids?" the president asked.

"Ready!" KC said.

The director led them from the office.

"What's in all these other rooms?" Marshall asked as they walked toward the elevators.

"We have staff meetings in this room every morning," Director Smiley said.

"The office next to it is where we put together the Ten Most Wanted list." He pointed to a third door. "And this one is the office of the Federal Witness Protection Program."

"What's that?" Marshall asked.

"When witnesses go to court for big trials, the criminals usually go to prison. Naturally, they're angry at the witnesses. So to protect the witnesses, the FBI offers them a new identity and a new place to live. That way the bad guys or their friends can't find them."

"Cool," Marshall said.

The president and the kids rode the elevator back to the lobby. A few minutes later, they stepped into the waiting car. "We're ready to go," President Thornton told the driver.

"Um, could we stop and get a pizza?" KC asked. "Seeing that box made me hungry."

The president laughed. "Me too," he said. He leaned forward. "Matt, please take us to the closest pizza place."

"What are you doing, KC?" Marshall whispered. "I know you, and I'd bet anything that you're not hungry. What's up?"

"I have a hunch," KC said, watching the traffic whiz by. "I think the pizza box is an important clue."

"Sir, would you like me to call ahead for the pizza?" the driver asked the president. "This traffic is pretty bad right now."

"Good idea," the president said. "Okay, kids, what do you want on the pizza?"

"Pepperoni!" Marshall said.

"Broccoli," KC added.

"I want cheese and mushrooms," the president said. "Got all that, Matt? Make it a large, please."

Matt called in the pizza order, and soon he pulled the car to a stop in front of 'Round Town Pizza. Inside the wide glass windows were booths, an old-fashioned jukebox, and a counter holding stacks of empty pizza boxes.

"It's under my name, sir," Matt said. "Would you like me to go in?"

The president smiled. "No, the kids can handle this deal," he said. He gave KC some money.

KC and Marshall hopped out of the car and entered the shop. The man behind the counter smiled. "Welcome to 'Round Town, best pizza for miles around!" he said.

"We're picking up a large pizza for Matt," KC told the man.

"Just pulled it out of the oven," the man said. "Let me box it up for you."

KC and Marshall watched as the man expertly slid the large pizza into a flat box. "That'll be twelve dollars," he said.

KC paid and picked up the box. "Do you know a pizza place that uses red boxes?" she asked the man behind the counter.

"Nope, most places use plain brown, like ours," the man said.

"Thanks anyway," KC said. Then she frowned. Now why was the pizza box bothering her? It wasn't just that it was red, not brown. What was it?

3
Fooling the FBI

When they walked into the kitchen, KC's mom was filling a vase with water at the sink. She had on a pretty yellow dress and high heels.

"Mom, why are you all dressed up?" KC asked.

The president set the pizza on the table. "Did I forget something?" he asked. "Are we going somewhere?"

"Yes, Zachary, you did forget something," Lois said, smiling. "We have to go to the New England governors' lunch."

President Thornton smacked himself on the forehead. "Bad president! When do we have to be there, Lois?" he asked.

Lois glanced at the kitchen clock. "We have twenty minutes. Kids, do you want to come along?"

"No thanks, Mom," KC said, rolling her eyes at Marshall. "*Bor*ing!"

"So we get the whole pizza to ourselves?" Marshall said as he peeked inside the box.

"You'd better save me some!" the president said. He rushed out of the room to change.

KC and Marshall sat at the kitchen table and each grabbed a slice of pizza.

"I have a cool idea," KC said.

"Me too," Marshall said. "Ice cream after this pizza."

"No, I want to get a greyhound for the president," KC said.

"What?" Marshall said. He nearly choked on his mouthful of pizza.

KC slapped him on the back until he stopped.

"Why get him a greyhound?" Marshall was able finally to ask.

"Because he wants one," KC said. "Did you hear him talking about it last night?"

"Oh yeah, when we saw that guy with the dog," Marshall said.

KC nodded as she nibbled her pizza. "While you were still sleeping this morning, I found a Web site on my computer," she said. "It's called adoptagreyhound.com. The place rescues greyhounds after they stop racing at tracks, then finds homes for the dogs. And I want to get one!"

"Awesome," Marshall said. "So where do you get them?"

"There's a dog track just outside D.C.," KC said. "It was listed on the Web site."

She patted her backpack. "I printed out the directions. Maybe we can check it out today. I need to go out anyway, to mail a letter to my dad," she said. "And we need to investigate this fireworks mystery some more. Something in the FBI building is real fishy!"

"*We* need to investigate?" Marshall said. "KC, in case you haven't noticed, the FBI is on the case!"

KC watched a long string of cheese droop down onto Marshall's chin. That cheese reminded her of something . . . what was it? Suddenly she jumped up.

"Marsh, I just remembered something!" KC said. "There was no pizza in that box!"

"What box?" Marshall asked.

"The box in the trash can in the FBI office," she said. "The inside was totally clean. No tomato sauce, no sticky globs of cheese. You said it yourself!"

Marshall stared at her. "So why was a never-been-used pizza box in the trash can?" he asked.

KC took a bite of her slice. "I don't know." She chewed slowly and concentrated hard.

"Maybe a pizza guy came to the FBI pretending to make a delivery," Marshall said. "Only instead of a pizza, he had fireworks inside the box!"

"But why?" KC asked.

"Beats me," Marshall said.

He reached for another slice. "But whoever it was went to a lot of trouble.

For one thing, there was a guard there."

"Yes, Joe Cellucci," KC said. Her eyes opened wide. "Marsh, he might know who brought the pizza box into the FBI!"

KC jumped up again and cleared the table, sticking the leftover pizza in the fridge. She grabbed her backpack and rushed out of the president's residence.

Marshall ran after her, gulping down the rest of his pizza slice.

Fifteen minutes later, they arrived at the FBI building, out of breath.

A guard in a dark uniform was sitting behind the counter, staring at a TV monitor. The doors were locked, but he looked up when KC tapped on the glass.

He walked over while pulling a wad of keys off his belt. He chose the right key, unlocked the door, and held it open. KC glanced at his name tag. It said JOE CELLUCCI.

"Hello, miss," Joe said to KC. "I saw you here earlier today. Er, what brings you back? Is the president with you?" He leaned out the door and checked down the street.

"No, not this time," she said. "But he's real worried about those rockets that went out the window last night. We want to ask you some questions, okay?"

Joe Cellucci looked at the two kids. He pulled on his nose and scratched his chin. "I guess," he said. "But I don't know anything about any rockets."

The kids followed Joe into the lobby. They sat in a couple of chairs meant for visitors.

"The president and the fire chief think someone in that office last night shot the rockets," KC said.

Joe shook his head. "That office was locked. No one was in the building but me and Mr. Rinkel," he said.

"Who's he?" asked Marshall.

"Lawson Rinkel, on the third floor, room 303," Joe said. "He's here every Friday night, working late."

"Did he order a pizza, by any chance?" KC asked.

Joe opened his eyes wide and nodded. "Now how'd you know that, miss?" he asked. "He gets one every Friday night, right at nine o'clock."

"Who delivers it?" asked Marshall. "I mean, which pizza shop?"

"Red's Pizza," Joe said. "They have a

red truck, and all their workers wear red shirts and caps."

"The boxes are red, too, right?" KC asked.

Joe Cellucci nodded.

"What did the delivery person look like?" KC asked Joe.

Joe closed his eyes for a second. "A guy about my height," he said. "Red shirt and baseball cap. Tinted glasses. Oh, and a tattoo of a leopard on his arm right here." Joe touched his right forearm.

"What color was his hair?" Marshall asked.

Joe grinned. "It was blond, and really long," he said. "In those braid things. Not braided braids like girls wear, just long and stringy-like."

"Dreadlocks?" KC asked.

Joe nodded. "That's it," he said. Then he chuckled. "By nine o'clock, I'm usually pretty hungry. When I smell that pizza, my stomach goes crazy. Mr. Rinkel always saves me a couple slices and drops them off for me when he leaves."

KC remembered the empty pizza box in the trash can. "Did he save you any pizza last night?" she asked.

Joe tugged on his nose. "Nope. Mr. Rinkel called on his cell and said he was waiting for an important call from London, so I should send the pizza guy up. Guy gets here, signs in, and I send him up. A little later, Mr. Rinkel calls my phone again. This time he says he never got his pizza."

"So the guy went up with a pizza box, but he never delivered it?" KC said. She stood up and started pacing back and forth.

KC looked at Marshall. "I'll bet the pizza guy set off those rockets," she said.

Joe shook his head. "That room was locked," he said.

"Do you know his name?" KC asked.

Joe shook his head. "Red's has a lot of delivery folks," he said. "I never saw this one before."

Joe snapped his fingers, then hurried over to the counter. He picked up the sign-in clipboard and carried it back to his seat. "He signed in," Joe said, flipping a page back. "Oh rats!"

"What?" asked KC.

"He didn't write his name," Joe said. He turned the clipboard so KC and Marshall could read what was there.

The sheet was laid out with a long line

for a name, then two short spaces to write what time you signed in and signed out. On the line for July 4th, someone had scrawled the words RED'S PIZZA.

"He signed in at nine o'clock, but he didn't sign out again," Marshall said.

Joe set the clipboard on his lap. "So you think this pizza guy came in just to set off those rockets?" he asked. "But why?"

"That's what the president wants to know," KC said, standing up. "Thanks, Mr. Cellucci. Come on, Marsh."

"Where are we going?" Marshall asked as he hurried down the FBI steps after KC.

"To Red's Pizza," she said. "I want to talk to the dreadlocks guy."

4

The Disappearing Pizza Guy

KC stepped into a phone booth and found Red's Pizza in the directory. "It's only a few blocks from here," she said.

They hiked it in less than ten minutes. The small pizza shop was easy to spot. It was painted bright red.

"Look," KC whispered as she and Marshall walked through the door. On the counter, dozens of red pizza boxes were stacked. On the front of each was a drawing of a pizza that had been turned into a smiley face. Under the picture were the words A SMILE IN EVERY BITE!

"Can I help you?" a woman behind the counter asked. She was wearing a red shirt and red baseball cap and had a plastic badge hanging around her neck with her picture. Her name tag said NIKKI.

KC had planned her story during the walk. "I'm trying to find one of your drivers," she told the woman.

"Why, was something wrong with a delivery?" Nikki asked.

"No, the pizza was perfect," KC said. She smiled at Nikki. "It's sort of a surprise. I don't know his name, but he has blond dreadlocks."

"And a tattoo of a leopard on his arm," Marshall added.

The woman looked at the kids. "None of our drivers has dreadlocks," she said. "And I don't remember a leopard tattoo on any of the guys, either. Are you sure it was a Red's Pizza driver?"

"Yes, I remember the box," KC said. She nodded toward the stack of boxes near the cash register.

"Well, I'm sorry, but your guy doesn't work here," Nikki said.

"I guess we were wrong," KC said, puzzled.

"By any chance, did you sell an empty pizza box to anyone?" Marshall asked.

"An empty box? Not me," Nikki said. "But I guess another cashier could have sold one. None of them are here right now, though."

The kids thanked Nikki again, then left.

"Something is weird," KC said. "Whoever brought a Red's Pizza box into the FBI building doesn't work for Red's Pizza. But he pretended he did by wearing the uniform."

"Well, he fooled Mr. Cellucci," said Marshall.

They passed the post office. "Let's go in here for a minute," KC said, pulling an envelope from her pack. "I have to mail that letter to my dad." KC's real father lived in Florida. She wrote to him or called every week and went to visit him a couple of times a year.

They walked up the steps and into the post office lobby. While KC dropped coins into a stamp machine, Marshall checked out the posters on the wall.

"Look," Marshall said. He pointed to some pictures. A small sign said that these men and women were the nation's Ten Most Wanted criminals.

"It's the Ten Most Wanted list," he said. "They're pretty creepy-looking. Mr.

Smiley told us they put the list together in the FBI building, remember?"

KC studied the ten faces, looking for some guy with blond dreadlocks. All the faces looked mean and sad. She turned away from the pictures and slid her stamped letter into a mailbox. "Okay, Marsh," she said. "Let's go."

The kids left the post office. In the distance, they could see the White House.

"Wait!" KC said, startling a woman taking a picture of her family. "Who knew that Red's delivered a pizza to the FBI building every Friday night?"

"I don't know," Marshall said.

KC looked at Marshall with raised eyebrows. "Joe Cellucci knew!" She pushed a street-crossing button and waited for the light to change.

"So maybe there was no pizza guy at

all," KC said. "Joe Cellucci could have made him up. Maybe Joe Cellucci was the one who shot off those rockets!"

"Why would he do that?" Marshall asked.

"Who knows?" KC said. "But that would explain why Mr. Rinkel never got his pizza."

Marshall nodded. "And Joe has keys, so he could've got into that room that was locked," he said.

The light changed and the kids crossed. "Joe Cellucci could've made up that whole story!" KC said. "No dreadlocks, no pizza delivery, no pizza at all!"

"I don't get why, though," Marshall said.

"I don't, either," KC said. "But I have a sneaking suspicion Joe Cellucci was up to something. We have to tell the president!"

5

Threatening Phone Calls

President Thornton and KC's mom didn't get back until late that evening. KC and Marshall were in the kitchen playing Go Fish when they rushed in. They looked upset.

"What's going on?" KC asked. She dropped her cards on the table.

The president sat down alongside KC and raked his fingers through his hair. "I can't believe this!"

Lois sat in the fourth chair. "Kids, there's a problem," she said. "Do you know anything about the Witness Protection Program?"

KC and Marshall nodded. "Mr. Smiley told us about it this morning. It's where people get a new identity," KC said.

"Right. Each person who goes into the program has the name of an FBI agent they can call if they have a problem," Lois explained. "Well, a few hours ago, one of the agents got a call from a man who's in the witness program. The man told his agent that someone called him, making threats. The witness had to come up with one hundred thousand dollars or the caller would reveal his new name and address."

"What that means," added the president, "is that, somehow, someone has managed to get that witness's phone number and real name. That information is top-secret!"

"The witness is in danger," Lois went

on. "He's being protected in the first place because he took part in a trial against someone who committed a crime. If this criminal finds out where the witness is, and his new name, he'll have someone go after him!"

The telephone rang and the president answered. "Yes?" he said.

When he hung up, his hand was trembling. "Another witness has been threatened," he said. "A woman who has been in the witness program for three years got a call an hour ago. A person told her to pay one hundred thousand dollars or the whole world would learn where she is, and her real name."

"But how did this information get out?" Lois asked. "Only the FBI knows who's on that list, right?"

"I think I know how," KC said quietly.

The president looked at KC with raised eyebrows.

"I think the person who set off those fireworks in the FBI building last night stole the phone numbers," she said. "And I think it's Joe Cellucci, the guard."

Then KC and Marshall told the president and Lois what they learned from Joe Cellucci earlier that day. And how they went to Red's Pizza to talk to the man who delivered the pie.

"But we found out there is no such man," KC said. "So we think Joe Cellucci is lying, and *he* set off those fireworks."

"And in the confusion, he hacked into the computers!" Marshall added.

The president didn't look convinced. "I don't know," he said. "Those computers

are complicated. The hacker would have to have a lot of computer knowledge."

"Joe Cellucci could know a lot about computers," Lois said. "The building would have been empty, so no one would bother him when he did his dirty work."

"Well, not quite empty," Marshall pointed out. "Mr. Rinkel was there."

"Who?" the president asked.

"He works there," KC said. She explained to the president about how Mr. Rinkel stayed late on Friday nights and always ordered pizzas.

"That's interesting," the president said. He picked up the telephone and called the FBI director. "Please bring in Joe Cellucci, the guard in the FBI building, first thing tomorrow morning," he said. "And a Mr. Rinkel, who also works there."

The president looked at his watch. "I want to see them in the Map Room at nine o'clock sharp!" he said.

While the president was on the phone, KC grabbed Marshall by the arm. She pulled him to a corner of the room.

"Marsh!" she whispered. "We have to find a way to hear that conversation!"

6

Two Suspects

At ten minutes to nine, Marshall and KC were hiding behind the velvet drapes covering the Map Room's tall windows.

"What are we doing here?" Marshall hissed.

"Don't you want to hear what goes on?" KC made a crack between the drapes and peeked out.

Marshall shook his head. "We're spying on the president!" he whispered. "We could be sent to Siberia or something!"

KC grinned. "He might send *you* to Siberia, but not me," she said. "I'm his stepdaughter."

"Yeah, well, I'm not go—"

KC put her finger over her lips. She pointed toward the door as it opened. The president entered, followed by the FBI director, Joe Cellucci, and another man.

KC nudged Marshall. When he looked at her, she mouthed, "That must be Mr. Rinkel!" The president sat first, then Joe and the other man took their seats.

"Go ahead, please," the president told the FBI director.

"Mr. Cellucci, were you on duty the night before last?" the FBI director asked.

"Yes, sir, I was," the guard said. "From three until eleven."

"Good. Now tell us, how many other people were in the building during those hours?"

"Just me and Mr. Rinkel," he said.

"No one else came in at all?" the FBI director asked.

"Well, the pizza guy came at nine o'clock," Joe Cellucci said.

"Who was the pizza for?" the president asked.

"It was for me, Mr. President," Lawson Rinkel said. He was a short man with a round belly. His gray suit matched his gray hair. He had a thin nose and small dark eyes that darted around.

Mr. Rinkel explained that he stayed late in his office every Friday, writing a novel. He always ordered a pizza at nine o'clock, when he took a short break to eat. Then he'd keep working on his book till around ten, when he left the building.

"I was waiting for an overseas call from London at nine o'clock," Mr. Rinkel went on. "I didn't want to tie up the phone, so I called Joe on my cell phone and told him to send the pizza guy up when he got there." Mr. Rinkel shrugged his shoulders. "The pizza never showed up."

"But the delivery guy came in at nine o'clock," Joe Cellucci said. "I checked his ID, he signed in, and I waved him toward the elevators. After about fifteen minutes, my phone rang, and it was Mr. Rinkel, asking where his pizza was. I told him I had sent the guy up. Next thing I knew, the fire department showed up. They said someone was firing rockets out of one of the upstairs offices!"

KC gave Marshall a look. "There was never a pizza!" she whispered in his ear.

"Mr. Rinkel, why do you work on your book in the FBI building?" the FBI director asked.

Mr. Rinkel blushed. "My house is too noisy, so I stay late after work. But just on Fridays. I use my own laptop, so I didn't think anyone would mind."

"What's your job?" asked the president.

"I'm a computer technician," Mr. Rinkel said. "I fix problems for the other computer workers."

"Did you see or hear anyone on your floor while you were busy on your laptop?" the president questioned.

Mr. Rinkel shook his head. "No, sir."

"And what time did you go home?" the FBI director asked.

"About ten-fifteen," he said.

"Did Mr. Cellucci see you leave?"

"No, he wasn't at his desk, so I just left," Mr. Rinkel said.

The FBI director looked at Joe

Cellucci. "You were away from your desk?" he asked.

"I guess I must've been in the restroom," Joe Cellucci said. "I don't remember." His face had turned red. He stared at his shoes.

There was a silence, and then the president nodded at the FBI director. The director turned. "Mr. Cellucci, I'd like you to come back to my office," he said.

"But I have to get back to work," Joe Cellucci protested. His face turned even redder.

"As of now, you're suspended until further notice," the FBI director informed the man. "And you'll have a chance to call a lawyer."

Mr. Cellucci gulped. "A lawyer? But I didn't do anything!"

"Please come with me," the FBI director said.

The two men left the room.

The president looked at Mr. Rinkel. "Thank you for coming in," he said. "Tell me, what is your novel about?"

"It's a mystery," the man said. "About spies in Washington."

"Sounds good," the president said as he walked Mr. Rinkel to the door. "Please send me an autographed copy when you get it published."

"I certainly will, Mr. President!" Mr. Rinkel said.

Behind the drapes, KC held her breath. She was afraid to peek out in case someone was still in the room.

"You two can come out now," the president said.

Marshall poked KC in the side. She poked him back. "Nice going," Marshall hissed. "Siberia, here I come!"

KC and Marshall stepped out from behind the drapes. The president was sitting in a chair, waiting for them.

"Did you hear what you wanted to?" the president asked.

Both kids mumbled, "Yes, sir."

"I'll let you off the hook this time, but I'm serious, KC. Please don't eavesdrop anymore," the president said. "Now go get some fresh air. It must have been pretty hot behind those drapes."

The president grinned, then walked out of the room.

KC and Marshall left the White House by the back entrance. They sat on a bench in the Rose Garden.

"That was terrific, KC," Marshall mumbled. "We just spied on the president!"

KC didn't say anything. She was frowning and her forehead was wrinkled in thought. "Marsh, I kind of feel sorry for Mr. Cellucci," KC said, after a moment.

"Yeah," Marshall said. "Mr. Cellucci seemed like a nice man, not a crook."

KC shrugged and dropped the subject. Then she looked at her watch. "You know, if we hurry, we can go to the dog track and pick out a greyhound before lunchtime."

"Sure, I think we've got this case wrapped up," Marshall said.

"It's weird," KC said as they headed off the White House grounds. "Usually, I feel happy when the bad guy is caught."

On Pennsylvania Avenue, they walked toward the subway station. While they waited for a train, KC studied the printout from the greyhound Web site.

Marshall was reading an advertisement for a company called Globe Travel. The large ad showed a map of the world. Across the top were small clocks showing what time it was in major cities.

"Look, when it's three o'clock in D.C., it's only noon in California," Marshall said. "They're eating lunch!"

KC laughed. "You just had breakfast!"

"What time is it?" he asked KC.

"Ten-thirty," she said. She lifted her eyes from the Web site printout and glanced at the small clocks that showed different time zones.

Marshall counted on his fingers. "This is so cool. It's ten-thirty here, but in Tokyo it's already eleven-thirty tonight!"

KC nodded. "They're thirteen hours ahead of us," she said. Then something made her check the time in London, England. It was three-thirty in the afternoon there.

"Marsh, do you remember Mr. Rinkel telling the president about that phone call he was expecting last night?" she asked.

"Sort of," Marshall said. "What about it?"

"He said he was expecting a call from London when it was nine o'clock here," KC reminded him. "That's why he used his cell phone to tell Mr. Cellucci to send up the pizza guy."

"So?" Marshall said. "He didn't want to use the FBI's phone because he was waiting for the call."

"But it would have been two o'clock in the morning in London," KC said. "A weird time for anyone to be calling the FBI, right?"

Marshall did some more finger math. "Maybe he thought it was five hours in the other direction. That would make it four in the afternoon in London."

"Except that's wrong," KC said. She pointed at the travel poster in the window. "London is five hours ahead of our time, not five hours behind. Besides that, the FBI must have more than one phone line. So Mr. Rinkel didn't have to use his cell phone to call down to the lobby."

Marshall shook his head. "I don't get what you're thinking," he said.

A brown train to Rockville came along and slowed in front of the kids.

"What I'm thinking," KC said as the train stopped, "is that Mr. Rinkel is lying!"

7

A Familiar Face

The ride to Rockville, Maryland, took a half hour. When they stepped off the train, KC was reading the printout again. "It says there's a shuttle bus to the dog track," she said.

KC and Marshall looked around.

"There it is!" Marshall said.

Parked next to the station was a purple van. The words RIVERBANK RACETRACK were painted on the side, over a picture of a racing greyhound. KC and Marshall ran over to it.

A man was sitting behind the wheel, reading a newspaper.

"Are you leaving for the track soon?" KC asked.

The man glanced at her with twinkly blue eyes. "Are you old enough to bet?" he asked.

KC giggled. "No, I'm going to adopt a greyhound," she said.

The man nodded. "Nice idea," he said. "Those poor dogs have a hard life. Do you have a big yard?"

Marshall laughed. "It's huge!" he said.

The man started the engine. "Have a seat, please," he said. "We'll be there in ten minutes!"

Soon the purple van drove through a gate under a sign that read RIVERBANK RACETRACK. The driver pulled up next to two white tents. In front of one of the tents, people were sitting and eating at

small tables. The other tent had a big sign over the entrance that read GREY-HOUND ADOPTION.

"Good luck!" the driver said.

"Thanks a lot," KC said. She and Marshall hopped out. Behind the two tents, the kids saw hundreds of people in grandstands around a large oval racetrack. Greyhound dogs were racing around the oval, and a man's voice was making announcements over the speakers.

Inside the adoption tent, a man and woman were working behind a table. Hanging from the top of the tent were posters of greyhound dogs. A large jar on the table had a sign taped to the glass. It said YOUR DONATIONS HELP GREYHOUNDS FIND GOOD HOMES. There wasn't much money in the jar.

A long, sleepy greyhound lay under the table. He looked up and blinked. Marshall kneeled down next to the dog and rubbed his head. The greyhound licked Marshall's hand.

KC walked over and dropped some change into the jar.

"Thank you!" the woman said. "Can I help you?"

"I'd like to adopt a greyhound," KC told her.

The woman glanced behind KC. "Are your parents with you?" she asked.

"They're home," KC said. "I wanted to get a dog for my stepfather as a surprise."

"I'm afraid that's not how we place our dogs," the woman explained. "In order to be sure the dogs go to good, safe homes, we have to know the whole family who will live with the dog. We check the homes thoroughly."

"Oh, I didn't know that," KC said.

"But we can put your name on a list," the man said. "We have another office in downtown D.C. If your parent comes in to fill out papers, we can get started with the process."

"That sounds good," KC said. "I can have my mom come in, and it'll still be a surprise for my stepdad."

"Great," the man said. "What is your name?"

"Katherine Christine Corcoran."

The man wrote down her name. "And your address?"

KC said, "1600 Pennsylvania Avenue, Washington, D.C."

Marshall giggled.

The woman and man stared at KC.

"Dear, that's the address for the White House," the woman said.

"I know, and that's where I live," KC said. "My mom is married to President Thornton."

"Goodness!" the woman said.

"So this dog would be for the president?" the man asked.

KC nodded. "He really likes animals. We already have three cats!"

The woman and man exchanged looks. "I'm sure we can work something out," the woman said, then handed KC a brochure and a business card.

"Thank you," KC said. She slipped them into her daypack. "How do we pick out a dog?"

"Usually, you would first view one of

our videotapes," the man said. "Then you'd meet the dogs, face to face, and choose the one you like." He smiled at KC. "But we might make an exception for the president."

"Awesome!" KC said. "I'll have my mom call today!"

She and Marshall left the tent. They didn't see the purple van, so they walked over to the restaurant tent and sat down at a table. A waiter came over with menus. "What can I get you?" he asked.

The kids each ordered lemonade.

"Got it," the man said.

"Did you see her eyes bug out when you told her your address?" Marshall asked.

KC grinned. "I wonder if they believe me," she said as the waiter returned with

71

two glasses of lemonade. He dropped straws and a slip of paper on the table and darted away again.

"Look, Marsh, isn't that Mr. Rinkel?" KC asked. She pointed her straw toward a man sitting at a nearby table.

"It looks like him," Marshall said. "Same pointy nose. I wonder what he's doing here."

Mr. Rinkel was tapping his spoon against a glass of water. He kept checking his watch.

A man wearing a lime-green tracksuit sat down at Mr. Rinkel's table. He had bushy black eyebrows and a mustache that looked like a fat caterpillar.

The waiter went over to their table. The man in the green suit said something, and the waiter wrote down the order.

The men were talking, their heads bent low. The waiter brought two cups of coffee, then left.

Suddenly the man with the black mustache slid an envelope across the table. Mr. Rinkel swept it into his lap.

KC stared at the man in the green suit. She squinted her eyes. "Oh my gosh!" she said, then clapped her hand over her mouth. She leaned across the table toward Marshall. "Marsh, that man talking to Mr. Rinkel," she whispered. "I think I saw his picture on the post office wall!"

"You're kidding me, right?" Marshall said.

"No! Look at him," KC said, keeping her voice low. "If you take away his mustache, he looks like one of those Ten Most Wanted guys!"

8

The Real Crook

Hiding their faces behind the lemonade glasses, KC and Marshall watched the two men.

"I wish we could hear what they're saying," KC said. "Let's move to a closer table."

"Forget it!" Marshall said. "That guy with the mustache looks really mean!"

The man in green threw some money down on the table, then he and Mr. Rinkel walked away.

"Should we follow them?" KC asked, jumping up.

"No!" Marshall said.

KC ignored him. She wanted to see where the men were going. She put some money on the table and grabbed Marshall's arm. Marshall took one last slurp and went with KC.

"Look, Marsh, they stopped at the dog-track betting window!" KC said.

"That's what people do here, KC," Marshall said. "They bet on the races."

KC and Marshall watched Mr. Rinkel open the envelope. He pulled out a hundred-dollar bill. KC got a glimpse of more bills in there. Lots more.

"Why would that man give Mr. Rinkel all that money?" she asked.

Marshall and KC stared at each other.

"Come on," KC said. "We have to call the president! I think they arrested the wrong man!"

"You think Mr. Rinkel is the one who's blackmailing those people for a hundred thousand dollars?" Marshall asked.

"Yes!" KC said. "Otherwise, why would he use a cell phone when he didn't have to? And why did he say he was waiting for a call from London when it was two in the morning there? And why didn't he get his pizza when he always got his pizza at nine o'clock? And, especially, why is he taking money from someone who might be on the FBI's Most Wanted list?"

KC found a telephone booth near the betting window. "Keep your eye on them!" she told Marshall. Her heart was racing faster than the greyhounds. Her finger shook as she punched in the phone number.

When the president answered, KC

blurted that she and Marshall had seen Mr. Rinkel talking with someone on the Ten Most Wanted list. She told him about the envelope full of money. The president talked for a minute.

KC listened, then hung up and turned back to Marshall. "What're they doing?" she asked him.

Marshall pointed to a row of seats. "Watching a race," he said. "What did the president say?"

"He and Mr. Smiley are on their way," KC said. "He said to stay put and not go near those guys!"

KC and Marshall found seats several rows behind Mr. Rinkel and the other man. Marshall watched the dogs racing in a blur around the track. KC kept her eyes on Mr. Rinkel. She bit her nails, looked at her watch, then went back to work on her nails. What was taking so long?

"Those dogs sure are fast!" Marshall said.

"I wish the FBI were as fast!" KC moaned. She checked her watch for the hundredth time.

Marshall grinned at her. "Calm down, KC," he said. "They'll be here soon."

When the race was over, Mr. Rinkel went to the betting window. He came back a few minutes later to join his friend.

More dogs were brought to the starting gates. At a signal, the dogs charged ahead, sprinting after a fake rabbit. Before the race was finished, KC felt a hand on her back. It was the president. Mr. Smiley from the FBI and two men in black stood behind the president.

"You made it!" KC said.

"Where are they?" President Thornton whispered.

She pointed.

"They're all yours, Desmond," the president told the FBI director.

Desmond Smiley and his two men walked slowly toward Mr. Rinkel and the man in green. KC couldn't hear what was said, but she did see handcuffs flash in the sunlight. A few minutes later, the two FBI agents led Mr. Rinkel and his companion away.

9

A Surprise for the President

The president sat down between KC and Marshall and pulled a picture from his pocket. He held it up for them to look at. "Recognize this guy?" he asked.

"It's the man with Mr. Rinkel!" KC said.

Marshall took the photo from the president to look at more closely. "Except he doesn't have a mustache in this picture."

"His name is Bart Framer," the president said. "One of the nation's Ten Most Wanted."

"I was right! We saw his picture in the post office," KC explained.

"What did he do?" asked Marshall.

"A lot," the president said. He ticked things off on his fingers. "Counterfeiting, forgery, and extortion."

"What's extortion?" Marshall asked.

"It means threatening people to make them give you money!" KC said.

"That's right," President Thornton said. "And Bart Framer is probably behind the theft of the Witness Protection Program's list. I'll bet a pickle he's the one who convinced Mr. Rinkel to do the dirty work."

Desmond Smiley joined them in the grandstands. He had a big, contented smile on his face. "Great work, kids," he said to KC and Marshall.

"Are they on their way?" the president asked.

"Oh yes. Rinkel sang like a bird even before we stuck them in the FBI van,"

Mr. Smiley said. "He's a gambler and has huge debts, so when Bart Framer came to him with a briefcase full of money, he listened. Framer wanted Rinkel to steal the Witness Protection Program list. With that list, he could extort money from hundreds of the witnesses on it."

"And Lawson Rinkel figured out how to get the list while pointing blame elsewhere," the president said. "He disguised himself as a pizza delivery man, slipped past Joe Cellucci, and hacked into the computers."

"Rinkel was clever," Mr. Smiley said. "He worked late Friday nights to set a pattern. Somehow, he managed to get a key. He wanted Cellucci to assume he was up there last night, but he wasn't. He was outside getting into his dreadlocks disguise.

That's why he had to use his cell phone to call Mr. Cellucci."

"I can't figure out why he said he was waiting for a call from London," Marshall said.

"He had to, in order to have a reason to call Mr. Cellucci on his cell phone," the president said. "Only he forgot that London time is ahead of ours. You guys figured that out!"

"So why did Mr. Rinkel shoot the rockets out the window after he hacked into the computer?" KC asked.

"To create confusion. Rinkel knew what Framer was planning to do with the list of names," Mr. Smiley said. "Once that first witness got a threatening phone call, Rinkel had to know the FBI would start searching."

"He planted that pizza box so you'd look for some mysterious pizza guy," the president added.

"But instead they blamed poor Joe Cellucci," KC said.

"Yes, I've already apologized and invited him to the White House as my guest," the president said.

He patted KC's hand. "And you two will get the FBI reward for finding Bart Framer!" he said. "What will you do with the money?"

Marshall looked at KC. They both nodded. "I think we'll give some of it to the greyhound fund," he said.

"Great idea!" the president said.

"I know," KC said. "Let's go by that greyhound adoption tent right now." KC and Marshall grinned at each other.

When they entered the tent, the woman behind the table stood up and smiled. "Hello, Mr. President, I heard you were at the track," she said. She held a leash attached to the collar of a beautiful silvery greyhound. "We would like to present you with Natasha. Someone told me you have a big yard and a warm heart for animals."

Grinning, the president took the leash. He gave Natasha a scratch on the head, for which he received a doggy lick on his hand.

The president gave KC and Marshall a searching look. "I wonder how she knew I wanted a dog," he said.

KC smiled at her stepfather. "Maybe there's a spy in the White House," she said.

Did you know?

Do you know what the letters FBI stand for? FBI is short for Federal Bureau of Investigation. But when President Teddy Roosevelt started the agency in 1908, it was called the Bureau of Investigation. In 1933, the name was changed to the Division of Investigation. Finally, in 1935, it became the FBI.

J. Edgar Hoover was the director of the FBI from 1924 until his death in 1972. He was the FBI's director under eight different presidents. Now, however, FBI directors may serve no longer than ten years.

Did you know that the FBI also uses dogs to help capture criminals? These dogs are trained to find bombs, drugs, stolen money,

and people. Dogs are a big help because they have forty-four times the sniffing power of humans. Some dogs can pick up a scent up to half a mile away!

In 1950, the FBI began a new program—the Ten Most Wanted list. It named the ten criminals that the FBI most wanted to find. The FBI offers rewards for information leading to the capture of any of its ten most wanted.

Would you like to be an FBI agent? First you have to graduate from college. Then you have to get special training at the FBI Academy in Virginia. FBI agents take classes in science, in law, and in how to conduct investigations.

About the Author

Ron Roy has been writing books for children since 1974. He is the author of dozens of books, including the bestselling A to Z Mysteries and Capital Mysteries. He lives where he was born, in a quiet part of Connecticut. When not working on a new book, Ron likes to teach his dog tricks, play poker with friends, travel, and read thrilling mystery books. You can visit Ron on his Web site at www.ronroy.com.